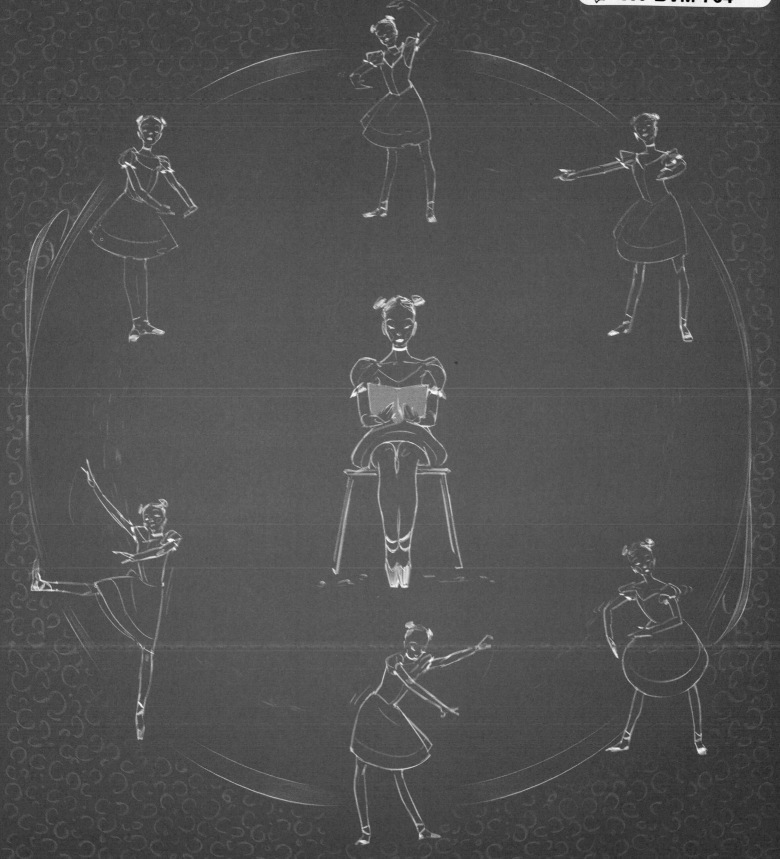

Bunheads

MISTY COPELAND

Illustrated by **SETOR FIADZIGBEY**

putnam

G. P. Putnam's Sons

G. P. Putnam's Sons

An imprint of Penguin Random House LLC, New York

Text copyright © 2020 by Misty Copeland | Illustrations copyright © 2020 by Setor Fiadzigbey

G. P. Putnam's Sons is a registered trademark of Penguin Random House LLC.

Visit us online at penguinrandomhouse.com

Library of Congress Cataloging-in-Publication Data
Names: Copeland, Misty, author. | Fiadzigbey, Setor, illustrator. | Title: Bunheads / Misty Copeland; illustrated by Setor Fiadzigbey. | Description: New York: G. P. Putnam's Sons, [2020] | Summary: A young Misty Copeland discovers her love for dance through the ballet of Coppélia. | Identifiers: LCCN 2020002297 (print) | LCCN 2020002298 (ebook) | ISBN 9780399547645 (hardcover) | ISBN 9780399547676 (kindle edition) | ISBN 9780399547652 (epub) Subjects: CYAC: Copeland, Misty—Fiction. | Ballet dancing—Fiction. | Coppélia (Choreographic work)—Fiction. Classification: LCC PZ7.C7887 Bu 2020 (print) | LCC PZ7.C7887 (ebook) | DDC [E]—dc23 | LC record available at https://lccn.loc.gov/2020002297 | LC ebook record available at https://lccn.loc.gov/2020002298

Printed in the United States of America
ISBN 9780399547645
10 9 8 7 6 5 4 3 2
Design by Eileen Savage | Text set in Carre Noir Medium
The art for this book was sketched and painted digitally.

This is for those who love to dance. Who dance because it gives you a voice, power, beauty, hope, and joy. You are all beautiful, and I celebrate everything that makes you unique. To all of my little Bunheads, dance your dance and live your dreams! —M.C.

To my wife, Maame, for always believing in me.
For my daughter, Lael, who always brings me joy. —S.F.

When Miss Bradley announced they'd
be performing the ballet *Coppélia* for
the recital, everyone in Misty's class shouted
excitedly and gathered around to hear their
teacher tell the story of Coppélia.

Misty didn't know what *Coppélia* meant, and she was too shy to ask—especially since it was her first ballet class ever! So Misty took a spot on the floor, and before she knew it, she was completely entranced as Miss Bradley told the tale.

Once upon a time, an odd old
toymaker made a beautiful
life-size doll named Coppélia
to cure his lonely heart.
The doll was so pretty and
looked so real that a boy
named Franz fell in love
with Coppélia at first sight—
even though he'd already told
Swanilda he would marry her!

Swanilda was furious when she caught Franz blowing kisses to Coppélia, but Franz ignored her anger.

Later, Franz sneaked into the toymaker's house to see Coppélia, but the toymaker caught him.

When the toymaker realized that Franz was in love with his doll, he had an awful idea. Maybe he could use Franz's love to turn Coppélia into a real girl!

Lucky for Franz, Swanilda had also sneaked into the toymaker's house out of curiosity, and she was still hidden inside.

She overheard the toymaker's evil plan and decided to dress like Coppélia to confuse the old man.

Once the toymaker believed that his doll had finally come to life, Franz escaped.

After that, Franz realized what a fool he'd been, and he married Swanilda.

The two lived happily ever after.

Misty loved how Swanilda never lost sight of her goal or her real love. She knew she wanted to be Swanilda.

"In just a few days, we will decide what roles you will dance in the performance," Miss Bradley said. "Now let's practice."

First there was a développé to tendu
front with one leg lifted forward, the
pointed foot gently touching the floor.

Next was the rond de jambe to tendu front, with the leg stretched straight out to the front, making big circles round and round in the air with the toes.

Then it got a bit harder with the pas de bourrée, moving from side to side as one foot crossed over the other.

They had such fun with the soutenu as the young dancers twirled and spun in unison.

Finally, the lesson ended with simultaneous pas de bourrée, again and again. Misty picked up the steps easily, following only a half second behind the rest of the class.

"Have you ever danced *Coppélia*?" Miss Bradley asked.

Misty shook her head, nervously replying, "I've never taken ballet before."

"Well, you're very good," Miss Bradley said.

"Come," she called to Misty and Cat, a younger girl who was full of energy. "You two, up front."

Misty could feel her heart pounding. Miss Bradley asked
Cat to show Misty the dance of Coppélia.

Coppélia sits in a chair on the balcony of the toymaker's
house throughout the first act of the ballet.

Cat held her arms in first position, then lifted her arms and turned her head like a robot, up and down and side to side. She performed the moves beautifully.

When it was Misty's turn, she imitated Cat from memory. "You are both very gifted," Miss Bradley said.

As soon as Misty got home, everything about the new class and the *Coppélia* fairy tale tumbled out of her.

"I'm proud of you," Mommy said.

Misty was so excited, she could hardly sleep.
She lay in bed thinking about the doll coming to
life. Misty said her name aloud: "Co-*pay*-lee-ah."
It felt magical and full of mystery!

The next day, Misty arrived early. Cat was there, too, dancing the steps of Swanilda. Oh no! Misty didn't know if she could compete with someone so talented.

Soon Miss Bradley arrived.
"Do you girls know which part
you want to play in the recital?"
Misty held her breath as Cat
answered, "Coppélia."

When the other dancers arrived, filling
the studio with laughter, Misty and Cat
stayed close, learning from each other.

Cat's movements were
sharp, while Misty's were soft.
They tried to copy each other's
style until they were giggling.

At last, Miss Bradley was ready to audition the dancers to cast the parts that everyone would play in *Coppélia*.

Nearly all hands shot toward the ceiling to audition for Coppélia. Misty was nervous for Cat. But when Cat began to move, Misty knew no one would be able to outdance her.

When it was time to dance the role of Swanilda, Misty was paired with a grinning younger boy named Wolfie, who was portraying Franz. Wolfie was on a mission to catch Misty's attention.

The next day, Miss Bradley announced who would play what parts. Misty was excited when Cat got the part of Coppélia, and even happier when she won the part of Swanilda.

The next few weeks were full of hard work for Misty. She had to perform both Swanilda and Coppélia when she tricked the toymaker into thinking she was the doll who had come to life. It was a lot to learn.

Watching Cat dance her parts
with ease made Misty try harder.
They inspired each other.

The night of the performance,
Misty was so excited, she couldn't
keep still. Staring up at the heavy
red curtain, Misty felt a hand on
her back.

"You okay?" Cat asked.

Misty nodded. "I'm ready."

And then the curtain was rising up
and away. Bright spotlights spilled onto
the stage, casting a spell of stillness that
would only be broken by movement.

In her tutu and braided bodice, Misty pranced onto the stage as Swanilda, with Wolfie playing the part of Franz.

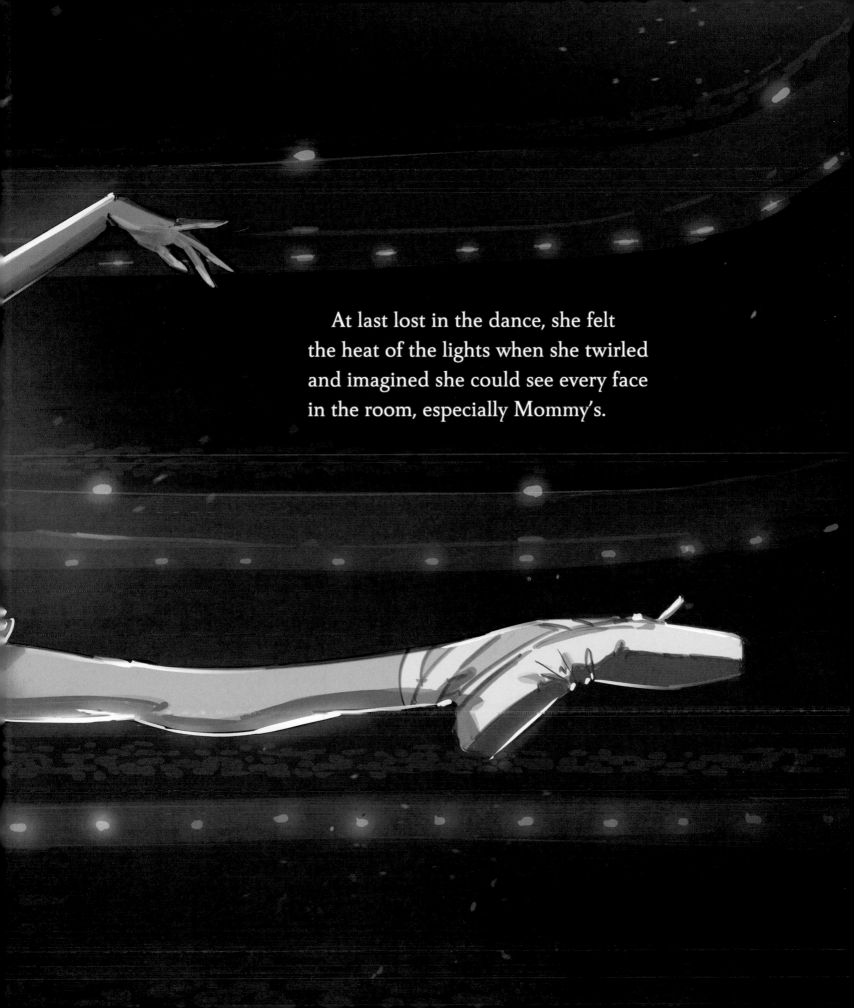

At last lost in the dance, she felt
the heat of the lights when she twirled
and imagined she could see every face
in the room, especially Mommy's.

Misty smiled, proud of what she, Cat, Wolfie, and all the other dancers had accomplished together. She couldn't wait to see what they would do next.